FROM HEAVEN TO EARTH

FROM HEAVEN TO EARTH

GEORGIA STARKE WOOLRIDGE

ReadersMagnet, LLC

From Heaven To Earth
Copyright © 2020 by Georgia Starke Woolridge. All rights reserved.

Published in the United States of America
ISBN Paperback: 978-1-952896-59-0
ISBN eBook: 978-1-952896-60-6

All rights reserved. No part of this publication may be reproduced, stored in a retrieval system or transmitted in any way by any means, electronic, mechanical, photocopy, recording or otherwise without the prior permission of the author except as provided by USA copyright law.

The opinions expressed by the author are not necessarily those of ReadersMagnet, LLC.

ReadersMagnet, LLC
10620 Treena Street, Suite 230 | San Diego, California, 92131 USA
1.619.354.2643 | www.readersmagnet.com

Book design copyright © 2020 by ReadersMagnet, LLC. All rights reserved.
Cover design by Ericka Obando
Interior design by Shemaryl Tampus

Contents

Dedication.............................. vii

The Beginning 1

The Decision–Heavenly Love 9

The Birth– 11

Dedication

This book is dedicated to my youngest granddaughter, Yasmeen. You have brought so much joy to me since your birth. You have a beautiful heart, you are the heroine of your own story and I am inspired as you continue to flourish. Grow in spirit, grow in love, grow in kindness and remember always to treat others the way you would like to be treated. Stay true to yourself, be smart, be honest and most of all be loving.

I love you.
Grandma

The Beginning

One day God was walking around in His Heaven  looking down at His Earth. He did this every day and each time a little Petal would fly and land on His shoulder. He knew this, He had seen it many times. He spoke to it and asked, "how are you?" He knew the couldn't speak, but since He was **All Knowing,** He knew the was feeling sad. He strolled through the beautiful garden  gazing down and all He had made, the still on His shoulder.

With His attention still on Earth 🌍 He saw children playing 🛝 and having fun. The children were dressed in beautiful colors and hues. Again, He read the 🔴 mind and as it asked "who are they, what are they doing? What are they doing?" He replied, "those are my children they 🎈 are playing".

Again, He felt sadness from the  for it had never experienced anything like that. It wanted to be His child; it did not know it already was. Then He heard the women voices calling to the children and again, He felt the  asked "who are they?" He replied, those are the  mothers of the children.

He looked at the  and felt its thoughts, "I wish I had a mother".

The children went into their different homes , washed  their hands and gathered  around the table.

Later a man  joined the children at the table. They bowed their heads. The  asked, "what's happening, what are they doing?"

God said they are giving thanks  for the meal they are about to receive.

Later the asked, "who is that?" God replied that is the father. Children have parents, called a mother and a father  also called a mom and a dad. He explained that their duty is to nurture, provide, love, shelter and guidance to the children during their young lives.

The 🍃 was so amazed and also very sad, it wished for a mom and a dad.

The next day God was walking in His Heaven 🏞 and again the 🍃 came and landed on His shoulder, sad, and very lonely. He asked, "why are you so sad? Why are you so lonely?" He knew, but He wanted to hear it explained.

The  said, "I've never had children to play with, I've never had a mother and a father, and I also want to give thanks." He asked lovingly "would you like to have one?"

He felt the  answer, "yes, oh yes!"

The Decision—Heavenly Love

So God decided to plant the . He chose a father and mother  so that the  could experience earthly love, not just heavenly love but an earthly life also. He said you will have a family, a big family. You will have many people to love and adore you as I have. You will have good times and bad times but remember, I will always be here for you.

The Birth—

And so the  was born. It weighed 6lbs. and 7ozs. The parents  were so happy and thankful that God had blessed them with a baby .

It had been born into a big family   , with a sister, grandmothers, great grandmother, great grandfather, cousins, uncles and aunts, etc. It was no longer a petal, it was a real person, it was truly happy. The parents decided to name the baby, YASMEEN.

And God looked down from His Heaven  and smiled;
And said "Well Done"  .